Catch
the Red Bus!

For Nicholas and Tom

Julia Killingback

Methuen Children's Books

"Hurry up!" says Mrs Bear.

"We're going on our trip today."

"Are you ready?" asks Mr Bear.

"Let's play a colours game!"

What colour is the car?
It's **blue**!

Time to be off – what fun!
Brmm, brmm! Brmm, brmm!

What colour is the bus?
It's **red**!

Catch the red bus, hurry, let's ring!
Ding-ding! Ding-ding!

What colour is the cart?
It's **yellow**!

Gee up, don't stop!
Clippity-clop! Clippity-clop!

What colour is the train?
It's **green**!

Who'll be first to see the sea?
Diddle-de-dur, diddle-de-dee!

What colour is the boat?
It's **white**!

All aboard, wait for the hoot!
Toot, toot! Toot, toot!

What colour are the bikes?
They're **orange**!

Pedal safely out of town.
Up down, up down!

What colour is the plane?
It's **purple**!

Fly high in the sky,
Zoom, zoom! Zoom, zoom!

 What colour is the taxi?
It's **black**!

Time to go back home to sleep.
Peep, peep! Peep, peep!

PHOTOS OF OUR TRIP

car

bus

cart

train

The bears play a colours game
before they go to bed.

boat

bikes

plane

taxi

Can **you** find all the colours?
What is yellow, what is red?

"Good night."

First published in Great Britain 1985
by Methuen Children's Books Ltd, 11 New Fetter Lane, London EC4P 4EE
Copyright © 1985 Julia Killingback
Reprinted 1985 and 1986
Printed in Singapore
ISBN 0 416 49240 I